Follow Your Dreams

Robert Laberge/Getty Images

Jamie McDonald/Allsport

Imagine flying high in the air, spinning faster than a ride at an amusement park, flipping over and over, and landing on a razor-thin blade on frozen water. Sound scary and exciting? Figure skaters feel this way every day.

Allsport

Skaters are usually moving. They hardly ever stand still on the ice. Figure skating is a mix of gymnastics, dance, and speed skating.

Phil Cole/Allsport

Skaters must be strong and flexible. They spend hours stretching and toning their muscles so that they can perform complex moves. Without determination and dedication, a skater cannot do well.

Skaters need to be fast in order to jump high off the ice. Their strong bodies come from eating right, getting enough sleep, and taking care of themselves. Skaters try not to eat a lot of junk food because eating healthy helps make their muscles strong.

Mike Powell/Allsport

Doug Pensinger/Allsport

To learn jumps, skaters must leap, turn, and fall over and over again until their bodies learn to go higher and faster. They must also learn to land safely. As time goes on, skaters learn to spin more times with each jump. They flip, twist, and turn higher than ever before.

Gliding across the ice with the presence of a ballerina, skaters are judged on their form, posture, and grace. Even a small bend or lean can make a skater fall on the ice. Ouch!

Rick Stewart/Allsport

Between jumps and spins, skaters perform **connecting elements** such as turns. They use either one foot or both feet each time. Often, skaters use their turns to draw figures in the ice. This is how the sport got its name.

Becoming a champion figure skater requires training, practice, and perseverance.

Chris Cole/Allsport

Jamie McDonald/Allsport

When skaters compete, they perform two types of programs. These are called **compulsory** and **free.** In the **compulsory program,** each skater must complete jumps, spins, and turns in a certain time period. There is little creativity allowed in this part of the competition. Yet, each skater tries to make his or her routine unique.

In the **free program,** skaters choose music and costumes that fit their routine. Skaters try to engage the judges and the audience so they will like the performance. Each performance is like a mini-play. The routine is meant to showcase the skater's jumps, leaps, spins, and speed. If you were to plan a routine, what kind of music would you choose?

Brian Bahr/Allsport

11

Brian Bahr/Allsport

Figure skaters can perform alone or in pairs. Skating in pairs requires teamwork. Both skaters must perfect their timing and rhythm. Coordinating their moves, spins, and jumps requires patience. There are times when it can be frustrating if the skaters are not in sync. To be a champion, skaters must get over their fears of falling down, getting hurt, or making a mistake.

Brian Bahr/Allsport

When dancing in pairs, skaters use difficult movements. These include **lifts, throw jumps,** and **death spirals.** Sometimes, the female skater spins with her head inches from the ice. Other times, she flies 8 feet (2.4 meters) in the air, but she is certain that her partner will catch her on her way down.

Jed Jacobsohn/Allsport

Some of the moves skaters perform have strange names. For example, **Mohawk** and **Choctaw** are the names of turns. If you watch carefully, you will see skaters put their bodies in the shape of the letter "T." This is called the **camel spin.**

Jumping high is an important part of skating. Jumps also have strange names. The most popular jumps are the **axel, loop, salchow,** and **lutz.** The type of the jump is based on its take-off and landing positions. Some jumps begin with the skater moving forward or backward and on different edges of the blade.

Brian Bahr/Allsport

Skaters come from countries all over the world to compete. They come from different backgrounds and cultures. They often become friends. When skaters compete, they want to be the best. But, they cannot be afraid to lose. True champions learn to win or lose with grace and pride. Although, nothing beats the feeling of success when a skater's hard work and dedication is rewarded with a medal!